Enid Blyton ™

The Clockwork Kangaroo

Illustrated by Pam Storey

Published by
Grandreams Limited
435-437 Edgware Road
Little Venice
London W2 1TH

Printed in Hong Kong

The toys in Jackie's playroom were very happy together till the clockwork kangaroo came. Jackie had a big brown bear on wheels, a horse and a cart, a sailor doll, and a few other toys who lived together in the toy cupboard.

At night the sailor doll took the horse out of the cart, so that he could run free. In return the horse gave the doll a ride round the playroom. He loved to gallop about, and his hooves made a tiny pattering noise on the floor. Once when Jackie woke up, he heard the noise, but he thought it was the rain pattering outside! If he had looked into the playroom he would have seen that it was the horse.

The bear got the sailor doll to oil his wheels so that he could run quietly about at night without making any noise. The train didn't make much noise because it didn't run on its rails at night, but just anywhere it liked on the carpet.

And then the jumping kangaroo came. It was a very clever toy really, because its clockwork made it jump high in the air just as a real kangaroo does. How it could jump!

"Hallo!" said the kangaroo, the first night. "How are you all? I'm a jumping kangaroo."

"Oh, really, how interesting!" said the bear politely. "How far can you jump?"

"I'll show you," said the kangaroo. He sprang high into the air - and landed, bang, on the bear's nose!

"Please don't do that again," said the bear crossly, shaking the kangaroo off his nose.

The kangaroo sprang high into the air once more - and this time he landed on the engine of the train with such a crash that he bent the little funnel.

"Look what you've done!" said the train angrily. "I was very proud of my funnel. Now you've spoilt it. I don't look like a real train any more!"

The kangaroo leapt about till his clockwork was run down. Then, because no one would wind him up, he sat in a corner and sulked. He just couldn't reach his own key with his paws, which was a very good thing.

He made friends with Sam, a tiny doll whom nobody liked very much, and Sam was always ready to wind him up. After that the toys didn't have a very good time at night, for the kangaroo was always jumping out at them from somewhere.

"He really is a nuisance," said the bear rattling his four wheels crossly.

"So is Sam," said the sailor doll. "Always winding up the kangaroo so that he can jump on us."

"I wish the kangaroo had never come to our playroom," said the train. "We were as happy as could be before."

"Can't we get rid of him?" asked the horse. "Last night he jumped on my back and frightened me so much that I galloped three times round the playroom with him without stopping - and then he grinned and said, 'Thanks for the ride!' Horrid creature!"

"Toys!" groaned the kangaroo. "Help me. I'm sorry I ever annoyed you. Do, do help me."

The toys were so pleased to think that the kangaroo was back that they all rushed to help him. They washed him. They brushed him. In fact, they couldn't do enough for him, and he almost cried for joy.

"It was dreadful in the dustbin," he said. "Really dreadful. Don't send me there any more. I'll never behave so badly again."

She bent down and picked up the kangaroo. "Well, if it isn't the clockwork kangaroo. He must have got in here by mistake. I'll take him back to the playroom."

She took him back. Jackie wasn't there, so she put the dirty, cindery toy on the floor and left him there. He groaned, and the toys peeped out at him. At first they didn't know who it was, for the kangaroo was so dirty and so spotted with tea-leaves.

"If only I had just one more jump left!"
sighed the kangaroo sadly. "The next time
anyone takes the lid off the dustbin I could
jump out, for I am near the top."

Just as he spoke, Jane came to put some
cinders there. She took off the lid and emptied
the pan of cinders all over the kangaroo. He
gathered himself together and did one last
jump. Out he leapt - and Jane gave a yell.

"My gracious! What's this leaping about?"

Well, the night went on, and the morning came - and Jane came to clean the playroom. She carried away the basket to empty it into the dustbin. And then the toys began to feel rather dreadful.

"I don't much like to think of Kangaroo in the smelly old dustbin," said the sailor doll. "What happens to things in the dustbin?"

"I don't know," said the bear. "Do you think he is very unhappy?"

Certainly the kangaroo was most unhappy. Jane had emptied him into the dustbin, and he had fallen on to a pile of wet tea-leaves, which stuck all over him.

He began to scramble round and round
the basket, like a goldfish swimming round a
bowl. The toys giggled. The kangaroo had
often frightened them - and now he was
frightened himself. He would know what a
horrid feeling it was.

Sam felt sorry for his friend, but he
couldn't do anything to help him. "Oh, Kangy,
I think the other toys have done this on
purpose," he said sadly. "They have punished
you for being naughty to them."

"My clockwork is nearly run down," he cried. "I hate being mixed up with apple-peel, and paper, and dead flowers."

"Serves you right," said the bear gruffly. "You are a nuisance - and the right place for nuisances is the waste-paper basket or the dustbin."

The kangaroo began to cry. His clockwork had now run down and he could jump no more. He smelt of apple-peel. He was very unhappy because he knew that the basket was emptied into the dustbin every morning.

"I say! I've fallen into the waste-paper basket," called the kangaroo, trying to scramble out. "This is most extraordinary."

"Yes, isn't it," giggled the sailor doll. "Didn't you see it there?"

"No, I didn't," said the kangaroo, puzzled. "It just seemed to come underneath me. I say, help me out, somebody."

But nobody did. Sam was too small to help, and the others wouldn't even try.

The kangaroo tried to jump out. He leapt higher and higher - but the basket was tall and he just couldn't jump over the top. He began to get frightened.

The kangaroo jumped. My, he did jump well! The doll saw him sailing through the air as if he had wings - and then with a hard push the waste-paper basket was set right under the kangaroo - and he fell into it, plomp!

He was most surprised. He sat down on some apple-peel and torn-up paper and blinked his eyes in astonishment.

"What's this?" he thought. "What's this?"

"Got him!" said the sailor doll in delight. All the toys danced round the basket in joy, except Sam, and he was cross. But he couldn't do anything at all.

"Now's the time to catch him!" whispered the bear to the sailor doll. "Where's the waste-paper basket?"

"I've got it ready under the table," whispered back the doll. "I'll go and push it out just as the kangaroo jumps! Don't say 'one, two, three, jump' till I'm ready."

The sailor doll ran under the table to the tall waste-paper basket. He took hold of it, ready to push it out. The bear saw that he was ready and counted for the kangaroo. "Are you ready? Now, one, two, three, JUMP!"

"Goodness! What a noise!" said the bear.
"That wasn't a very good jump, Engine. Have
you hurt yourself?"

"No," said the engine, and ran off into a
corner on its six wheels to watch what was
going to happen. The sailor doll jumped next -
and his was a splendid jump, even better than
the ball's. The kangaroo was so impatient to
show that his jump would be even finer that he
pushed everyone else out of the way and stood
on the chalk-line himself, quite determined to
win the prize.

Sam stood on the chalk-line, grinning. He jumped - quite a good jump for such a tiny doll. The bear drew a chalk-line at the spot where he landed. "Now you, Ball!" he called. The red ball rolled up. It bounced off the chalk-line and did a very good jump indeed. The bear drew another line.

"That's fine, Ball," he said. "I believe you will win."

"No, he won't!" cried the kangaroo at once. "Let me try now!"

"It's not your turn," said the bear.

"Train, come on."

The engine ran up and stood with its front wheels on the chalk-line. It gave a puff and jumped - but it fell right over on to its side with a clatter.

"This is the jumping-off place," said the sailor doll, drawing a little line on the carpet with a piece of white chalk. "And we'll draw a white line to show where everyone jumps to - and the one who jumps the farthest shall win the prize."

"What is the prize?" asked the kangaroo at once.

"The prize is a chocolate," said the bear. The kangaroo was pleased. He wanted to have his turn first.

"No," said the bear. "Smallest ones first. Come on, Sam."

So he thought hard - and then he grinned at the others. He looked round to make sure that the kangaroo was not near, and then he whispered to the others.

"Listen!" he said. "Tomorrow night we'll pretend to have a jumping-match to see who can jump the farthest. And when it comes to the kangaroo's turn to jump, we'll quickly swing out the basket - and he'll jump right into it."

"Oh, good!" said the bear. "Let's do it."

So the next night the toys all began talking about a jumping-match, and, of course, the kangaroo came along in great excitement, for he felt sure that he would be able to win the match easily.

"I wish he'd jump into the waste-paper basket!" said the bear. "That's deep - and he couldn't get out of there."

"Then he would be emptied into the dustbin the next morning and that would be the end of him," said the sailor doll. "That's an idea!"

"What do you mean?" asked the bear.

"I'll think of some plan with the waste-paper basket," said the doll. "Don't speak to me for a minute."